Dear Parent:

Congratulations! Your child is taking the first steps on an exciting journey. The destination? Independent reading!

STEP INTO READING® will help your child get there. The program offers five steps to reading success. Each step includes fun stories and colorful art. There are also Step into Reading Sticker Books, Step into Reading Math Readers, Step into Reading Phonics Readers, Step into Reading Write-In Readers, and Step into Reading Phonics Boxed Sets—a complete literacy program with something to interest every child.

Learning to Read, Step by Step!

Ready to Read   Preschool–Kindergarten
• big type and easy words • rhyme and rhythm • picture clues
For children who know the alphabet and are eager to begin reading.

Reading with Help   Preschool–Grade 1
• basic vocabulary • short sentences • simple stories
For children who recognize familiar words and sound out new words with help.

Reading on Your Own   Grades 1–3
• engaging characters • easy-to-follow plots • popular topics
For children who are ready to read on their own.

Reading Paragraphs   Grades 2–3
• challenging vocabulary • short paragraphs • exciting stories
For newly independent readers who read simple sentences with confidence.

Ready for Chapters   Grades 2–4
• chapters • longer paragraphs • full-color art
For children who want to take the plunge into chapter books but still like colorful pictures.

STEP INTO READING® is designed to give every child a successful reading experience. The grade levels are only guides. Children can progress through the steps at their own speed, developing confidence in their reading, no matter what their grade.

Remember, a lifetime love of reading starts with a single step!

For Marissa and Gabriella
—T.R.

Copyright © 2010 Disney Enterprises, Inc. All rights reserved. Published in the United States by Random House Children's Books, a division of Random House, Inc., 1745 Broadway, New York, NY 10019, and in Canada by Random House of Canada Limited, Toronto, in conjunction with Disney Enterprises, Inc.

Step into Reading, Random House, and the Random House colophon are registered trademarks of Random House, Inc.

Visit us on the Web!
www.stepintoreading.com
www.randomhouse.com/kids

Educators and librarians, for a variety of teaching tools, visit us at
www.randomhouse.com/teachers

Library of Congress Cataloging-in-Publication Data
Redbank, Tennant.
A dozen fairy dresses / by Tennant Redbank ; illustrated by the Disney Storybook Artists.
p. cm.
Summary: With the Purple Moon Night Ball approaching, Hem, a talented seamstress, has big dreams of creating a beautiful new dress until all the other fairies ask her to make new dresses for them.
ISBN 978-0-7364-2663-3 (trade) — ISBN 978-0-7364-8080-2 (lib. bdg.)
[1. Fairies—Fiction. 2. Sewing—Fiction. 3. Clothing and dress—Fiction.] I. Disney Storybook Artists. II. Title.
PZ7.R24455Do 2010 [Fic]—dc22 2009028238

Printed in the United States of America   10 9 8 7 6 5 4 3 2 1

A Dozen Fairy Dresses

By Tennant Redbank

Illustrated by the Disney Storybook Artists

Random House 🏠 New York

Clink, clink, clink. Queen Clarion
tapped the side of her glass with a spoon.
She had something important to say.
Hem sat up straight in her chair.

"Three days from now is a special
night. It's Purple Moon Night," said Queen
Clarion. She looked at all the fairies sitting
around the tearoom. "When the moon rises,
it will be a deep purple. To honor it,
we will have a ball!"

Hem gave a happy sigh and closed her eyes. She could picture the dress she would make for herself. It would be pretty but simple. She'd be the belle of the ball!

Hem was a sewing-talent fairy. There was nothing she liked more than sewing a lovely dress. And a ball was the perfect reason to make a new one!

"Hem? Hem? Did you hear me?" a voice asked.

Hem opened her eyes. A group of fairies stood around her.

Tinker Bell shook Hem's shoulder.

"So will you do it?" Tink asked. "Will you make me a new dress for the ball?"

"And me?" Rani asked.

"And me?" Fira asked.

All the fairies wanted a new dress. Hem closed her eyes and sighed again. She loved making dresses, but she also liked to take her time. And she didn't have a lot of time before the ball! Still, she couldn't say no to her friends.

Maybe a ball wasn't such a wonderful idea after all.

As she flew back to her sewing room, Hem's head was spinning. She had to make ten dresses—in three days! How would she ever get them done?

She pulled a list out of her pocket. She had written down the kind of dress each fairy wanted.

Hem grabbed a basket and hurried to Lily's garden. Lily greeted her at the gate.

"Can I pick some flowers for dresses?" Hem asked the garden-talent fairy.

"Sure!" Lily said. "But only if you make a dress for me, too. I think a tiger-lily dress would be pretty!"

Hem shrugged. She already had to make ten dresses. One more couldn't hurt.

"Of course," she told Lily.

Lily and Hem picked the prettiest flowers in the garden.

They chose a red rose for Rosetta's dress

and a daffodil for Tink's.

They plucked pink sweet peas for
Rani's dress

and a striped white and purple crocus
for Silvermist's.

They found a pink tulip for Fira's gown

and a yellow pansy for Prilla's.

They chose a morning glory for
Beck's dress

and fresh green clovers for Fawn's.

Hem was surprised that Fawn even
wanted a new dress. She usually didn't like
to dress up!

Hem found bluebells for Bess and snowdrops for Iridessa.

"Wait!" Lily called out before Hem could go. "Don't forget the tiger lily for *my* dress!"

Lily looked at one flower. She looked at another. She wanted the perfect tiger lily. Hem tapped her foot. She didn't have time for this!

Finally, Lily picked the flower she liked best. She put it in Hem's basket. Hem's basket was heavy.

Hem slowly made her way to her room. Then she went to work. She cut. She pinned. She tucked. She sewed and sewed and sewed.

Soon it was dark. She had finished only three dresses!

Hem started again in the morning. There were so many choices to make! Would Tink like a long dress or a short one? Would Rosetta prefer puffy sleeves or plain sleeves?

Hem wanted all her friends to be happy. She sewed and pinned and cut. She finished Bess's bluebell dress at noon. Prilla's pansy dress was done two hours later. She finished Lily's tiger-lily dress by dusk. Hem stayed up late into the night.

Then it was the day of the ball. Hem
took in the waist of Fira's dress.

She added an extra ruffle to
Fawn's skirt.

She sewed a flower on Silvermist's top.
She was almost done. She had only two
more dresses to make!

Hem worked as fast as a bumblebee. Her fingers flew over the petals. Finally, the last dress was done. She hung it up next to the other ten.

Hem looked at the eleven dresses. Each one was different. Each one was lovely.

There was a knock on Hem's door.
She flew over and opened it. Her fairy
friends were crowded together outside.

"Are the dresses ready?" Prilla asked. She had an eager look on her face. The other fairies pressed forward around her. They couldn't wait to see their gowns!

"Yes! Come in!" Hem said. She waved the fairies inside.

Rosetta flew straight to the rose dress. "Oooh!" she cooed.

Tears came to Rani's eyes. She hugged her sweet-pea dress to her chest.

"What a dazzler!" Fawn said when she saw her green dress.

"Hem, you're the best!" Tink said. The fairies all took their dresses. Then they left.

Hem sank to the floor on a pile of petal scraps. She felt very good about all the beautiful dresses she had made. But she was tired. She didn't want to make another dress for ages!

Hem lay back and put her hands behind her head. Now she could relax. She could go to the ball in the courtyard and watch the Purple Moon.

The ball! Hem sat up straight.
She had not made a dress for herself!

Hem flew to her wardrobe. She opened the doors and looked inside. She had lots of pretty dresses. But none was as pretty as the ones she had just made.

Hem's eyes filled with tears. It was too late to find a perfect flower for her dress. She had wanted to be the belle of the ball. Now she'd just have to admire all the other fairies' dresses.

"Pins and needles!" Hem cried.
She kicked at the petal scraps around
her feet. A piece of a tulip drifted
off the pile.

Hem picked up the petal. Then she
spotted half a violet. She found a
tiger-lily scrap and part of a poppy.

Maybe she didn't need to pick a new
flower after all. She could make a dress
from the leftover bits!

Hem gathered up all the scraps of petals. She sewed and sewed and sewed. She poured all her talent into creating the dress. Her fingers were sore and her eyes were strained. Still, each stitch made her feel better.

It was dark out when Hem finished.
She slipped the dress over her head and
tied the back.

The dress swirled around her ankles
and floated around her arms. It felt
as light as air. Now a dozen fairy
dresses were done in time for the ball!

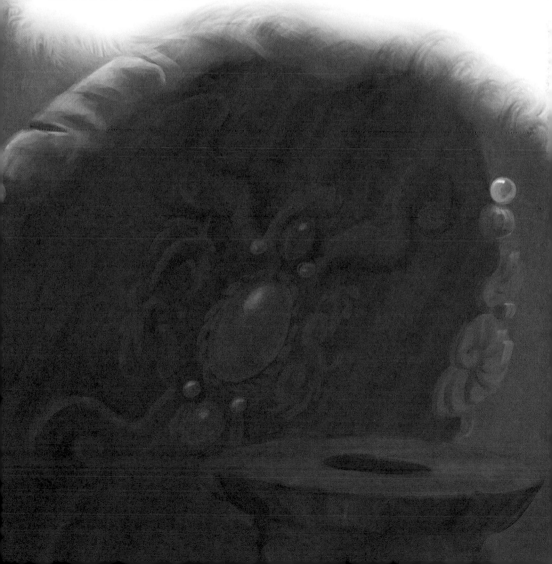

Hem flew to the courtyard. She stopped just outside. She stayed in the shadow of the Home Tree and looked up at the dazzling courtyard.

All her friends were there. They each wore a beautiful dress. Hem's heart swelled with pride.

Then Hem stepped into the firefly light.
The music stopped. The dancing stopped.
Every eye turned toward Hem.

Her dress was a rainbow of color.
It was red, yellow, orange, green, blue,
pink, purple, and white. The colors glowed.

Hem's friends quickly gathered around her.

"You look beautiful, Hem!" Silvermist said.

"It's all of our dresses pieced together!" Fawn pointed out.

"I'm happy that you made the best dress for yourself," Tink said.

Hem's glow turned pink all over.

Queen Clarion flew to her side.

"Hem, what a lovely dress!" she said. Then she whispered in Hem's ear, "Will you make me one just like it?"

A few hours earlier, Hem hadn't wanted to think of making another dress. But now she felt differently. Now she couldn't wait. "I'd be happy to!" she said.